The Custodian
from the
Black Lagoon

by Mike Thaler · pictures by Jared Lee

SCHOLASTIC INC.
New York Toronto London Auckland Sydney Mexico City New Delhi Hong Kong

To Matthew,
my son.

—M.T.

To Carole Inkrott,
dedicated teacher.

—J.L.

ISBN 0-439-18874-1
Text copyright © 2001 by Mike Thaler.
Illustrations copyright © 2001 by Jared D. Lee Studio, Inc.
All rights reserved. Published by Scholastic Inc.
SCHOLASTIC, CARTWHEEL BOOKS, and associated logos are
trademarks and/or registered trademarks of Scholastic Inc.

Library of Congress Cataloging-in-Publication Data available

10 9 8 7 6 5 4 3   01 02 03 04 05

Printed in the U.S.A.   24
First printing, August 2001

Somewhere in the dark caverns beneath our school lurks
the custodian.
His name is Fester Smudge.

I've never seen him because he waits until everyone's gone home before he emerges.

He knows all the secret passages and tunnels beneath the school — just like the Phantom of the Opera.

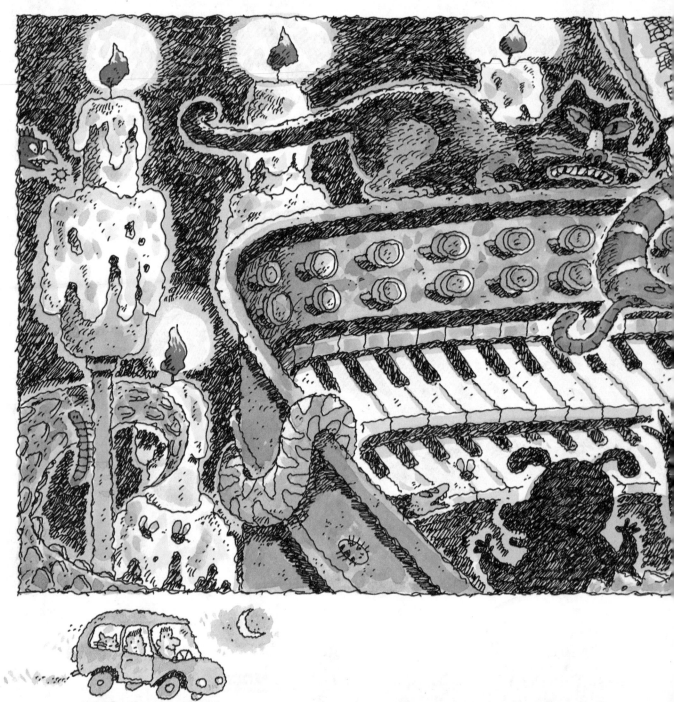

They say if you ride by after dark you can hear him playing
terrible tunes in his giant cave.

They say it's like Dr. Frankenstein's lab, full of machines that whirl, whizz, whirr, hum, crackle, and pop!

He's trained it to make the school boiling hot all summer...

and freezing cold all winter.
They say you can even ice skate in the halls.

Derek says Fester is mechanically challenged.

He changed a lightbulb and blew the ceiling off the gym.

Then he tried to fix a leak, and the cafeteria was underwater for a week.

Eric says Fester's grandfather was the engineer on the *Titanic*,

and his grandmother worked on the *Hindenberg*.

Kids are still talking about the time he electrocuted a visiting author with the clip-on mike . . .

and how the fire department came to free him from a folding chair . . .

and a Coast Guard helicopter came to rescue him from a toilet bowl.

Doris says he's not a very fussy cleaner either and
our school has been designated as the town landfill.

Freddy says flies follow Fester everywhere

Kids almost saw him the time he folded up the lunch
tables while everyone was still eating . . .

 or when he got his foot tangled in the rope and spent the day at the top of the flag pole.

Uh-oh, I can't remember my locker combination.
Here comes a man in overalls.
Oh, my, it's Mr. Smudge.

He has lots of keys on a ring, and he opens my locker.
Then he smiles, shines the handle, and walks away whistling.

Hey, he's really neat.
I'm gonna ask him if I can see his dragon sometime.